This Book belongs to

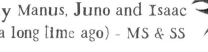

To Gremlins everywhere, especially Manus, Juno and Isaac
(who was promised a story book a long time ago) - MS & SS

For Alison, Bethan and Esme - IC

Thanks to Molly, Sara and Iain for coming on this monstrous journey with us.
Thanks once again to Dave Gray and Paul Croan.
Extra special thanks to Chank for the use of his wonderful 'WestSac' and
'Ballers Delight' fonts, see more at www.chank.com - LDB

Published by Little Door Books 2019
This edition published 2019

ISBN: 978-1-9999556-0-1

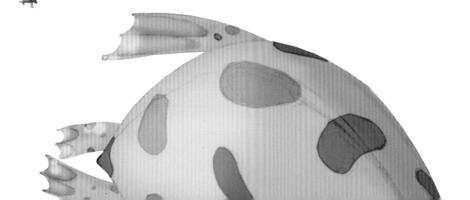

mail@littledoorbooks.co.uk
www.littledoorbooks.co.uk
twitter: @littledoorbooks

MONSTERS Unite

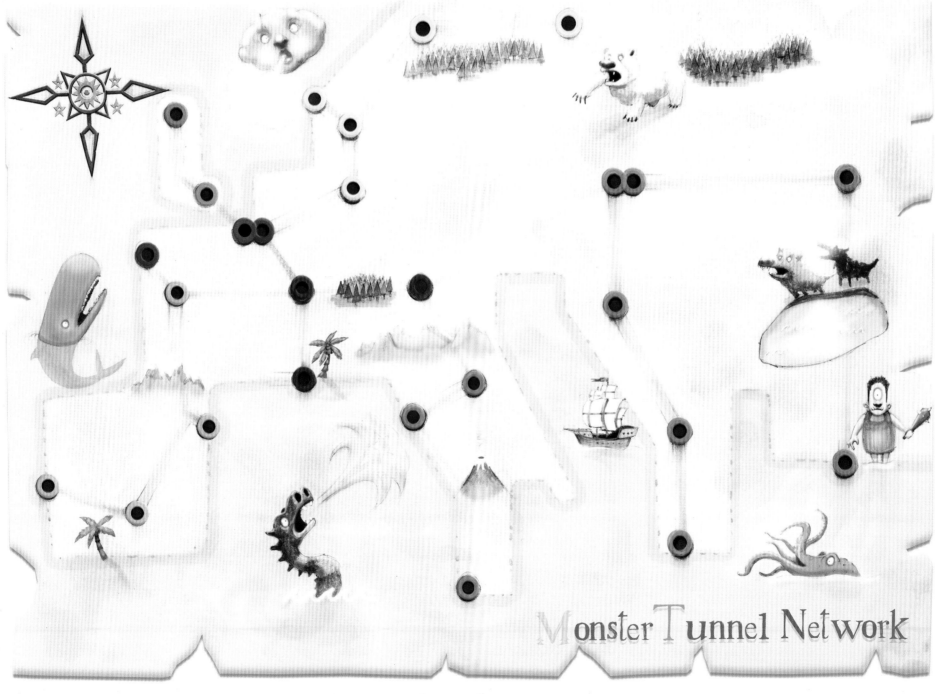

Monster Tunnel Network

Written by **Molly** & **Sara Sheridan** Illustrated by **Iain Carroll**

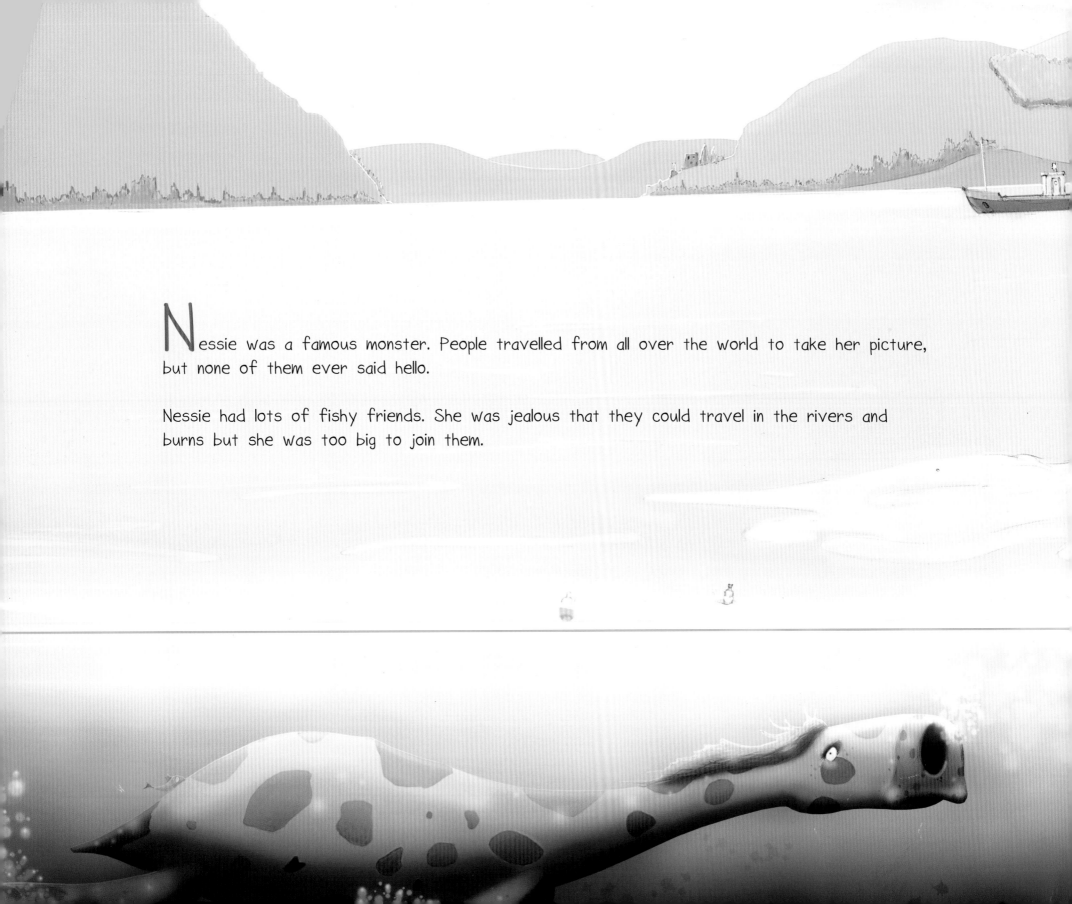

Nessie was a famous monster. People travelled from all over the world to take her picture, but none of them ever said hello.

Nessie had lots of fishy friends. She was jealous that they could travel in the rivers and burns but she was too big to join them.

The camera flashes
scared Nessie but
she hated the plastic
even more. It always
got in her way.

One day she decided
she'd had enough and
went to hide at the
bottom of the loch.

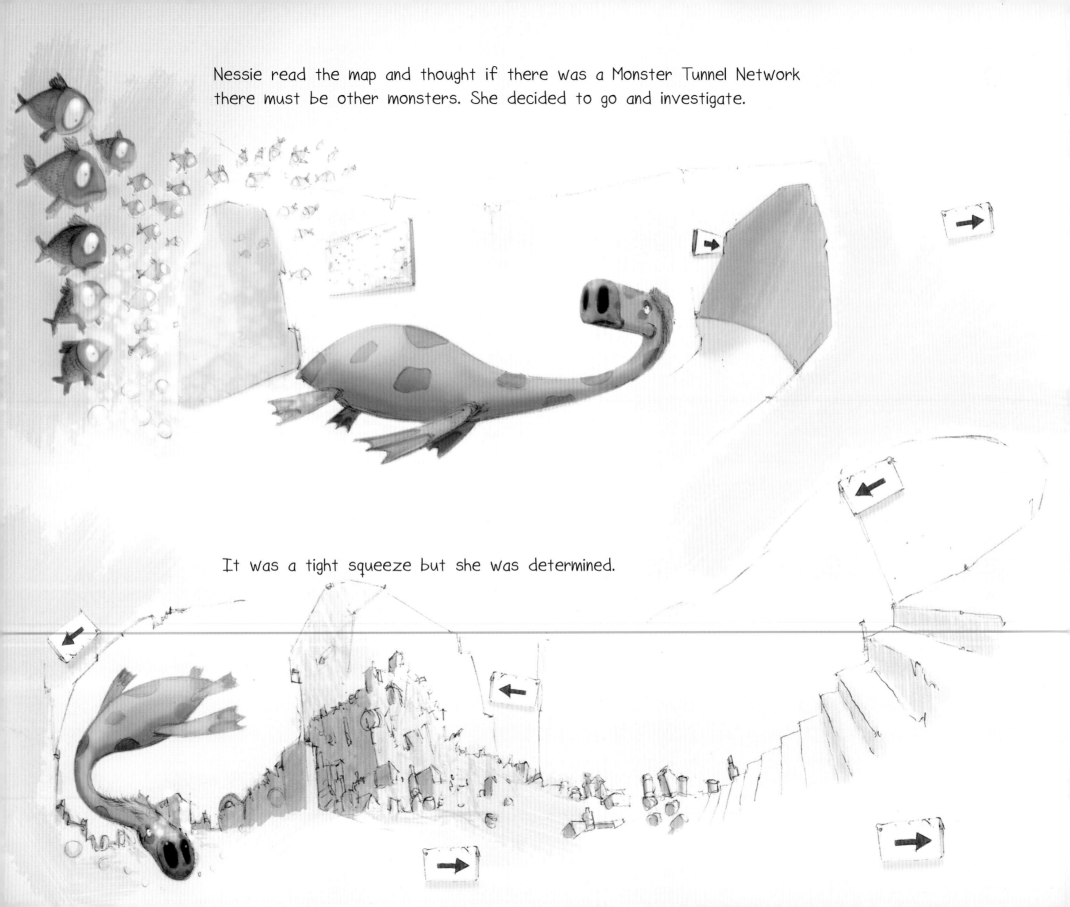

Nessie read the map and thought if there was a Monster Tunnel Network there must be other monsters. She decided to go and investigate.

It was a tight squeeze but she was determined.

The tunnel was dark and scary...

There was lots of squishy, shiny, strange fish she'd never met before.

...Finally Nessie found the way out.

EXIT
BEWARE!
TOXIC WASTE

"I'm Nessie," she replied. "I swam through the tunnel."
The Reverend Monstrosity looked worried. "Those tunnels have been closed for years."
"Well, I can't see why. Look, there's another one!" said Nessie excitedly. "Would you like to come with me and explore?"

"There is too much rubbish," the Reverend snapped and he wobbled away, rambling and ranting.
Nessie felt silly. But she took a breath and off she went.

EXIT

She's totally going to.

I bet she does.

Nessie almost got to the end of the tunnel but it was blocked
by a wall of rubbish.

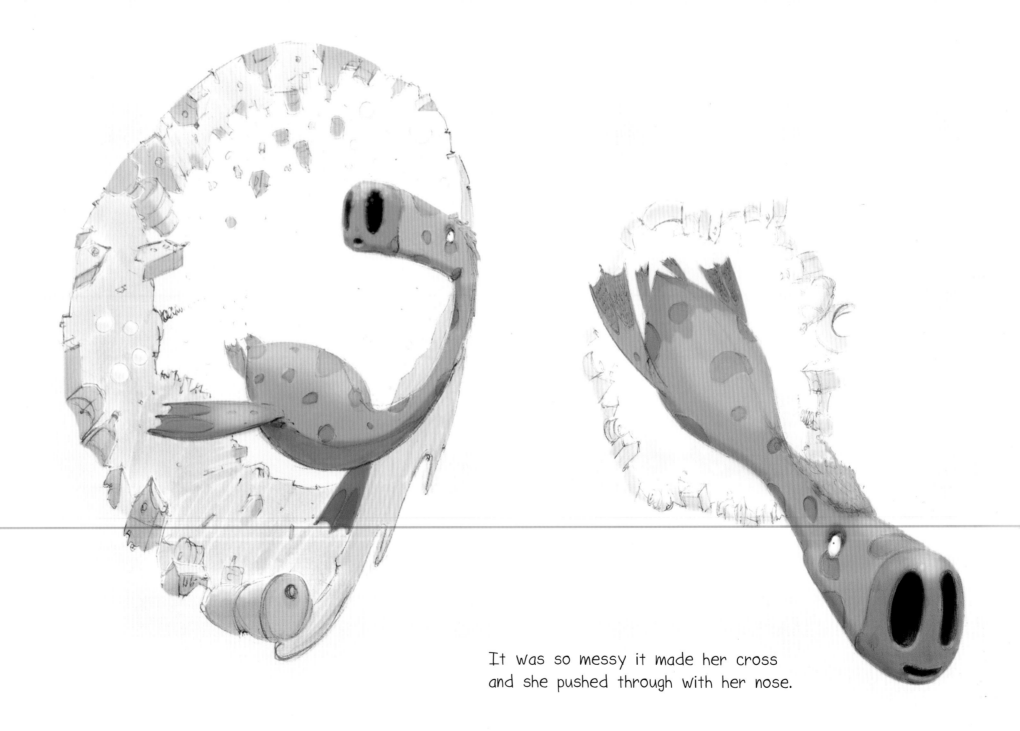

It was so messy it made her cross
and she pushed through with her nose.

Then with a crash the tunnel caved in behind her. How would she get home?
"Oh no, maybe the Reverend Monstrosity was right," said Nessie.

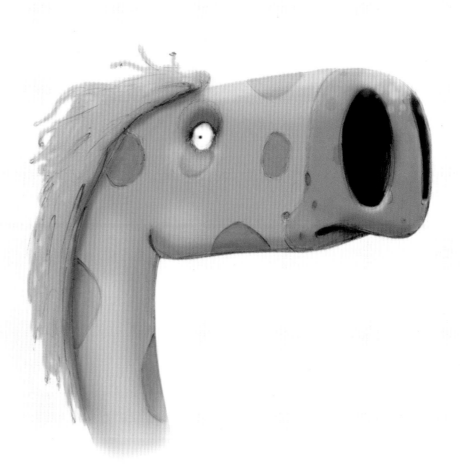

Then she heard a friendly voice...

"Hi there," it said as a new monster swam into view with a big smile.
"I'm Tay Tay. Come on in." Nessie didn't know what to say and suddenly she felt shy.
Tay Tay and Nessie talked for hours. Nessie told her new friend about the tourists
and that she was scared of not being able to get home again.

"There's always a way," said Tay Tay. "I've heard of a tunnel that might work for you. I'll come along. It's gonna be a great vacation."

Nessie was excited. She'd never been on an adventure like this and she'd never had a monster friend.

Going through the tunnel was much more fun together. At the other end they smelled something amazing, so they followed their noses.

Suddenly they were surrounded by a shoal of excited fish who served them a yummy meal. When they'd finished an elegant monster appeared.

Ooh la la!

"Welcome to my restaurant. I am Mais Oui," the elegant monster said.

Nessie explained she was trying to find a new way home.

"You MUST tell everyone to come and taste my wonderful food," Mais Oui said.

Nessie and Tay Tay promised they would.

..."Au revoir," Mais Oui smiled as she waved them off.

SORTIE

'le Beau Monstre'

Escal

Only half an hour for lunch?

At the end of the next tunnel it was very warm and sunny. A deep voice rippled towards them. "Senoritas, I am Pez. Are you lost?"

"We're looking for the tunnel going north," said Tay Tay. "My friend Nessie needs to get back to Scotland."

Pez was shocked. "Scotland? I'd take you but it's sooooo cold there."

"Cold? I don't do cold. Is it cold in Scotland?" asked Tay Tay.

"I'm used to the cold," Nessie said. "You should stay here and enjoy your vacation." Pez showed her the next tunnel and Nessie hugged Tay Tay goodbye. This time she wasn't scared to go on her own.

Adios new amigos.

Nessie travelled a long way on the Monster Tunnel Network.

I don't believe in this yeti you're talking about.

I can't stay, I've things to do.

ITALY

Switzerland

She passed through lots of different countries and met lots of new friends.

In the north
it was cold
and white.

Hallo. Who
are **you**?

Nessie met a huge furry monster.
"Are you a yeti?" she asked.
"No, I'm Templex. I'm an architect," he replied.
"Can you help rebuild my tunnel? It collapsed because of all the plastic."
"It's the stuff the humans leave behind," Templex explained.
"If we're going to fix it, we'll need help. I have some friends who can help us. Do you?"
"Yes," said Nessie. "And I know where to find them."

UTGANG

Where's her fur?
She must be freezing!

So off they went. As well as the monsters that Nessie had already met, loads more joined in. Everyone wanted to help.

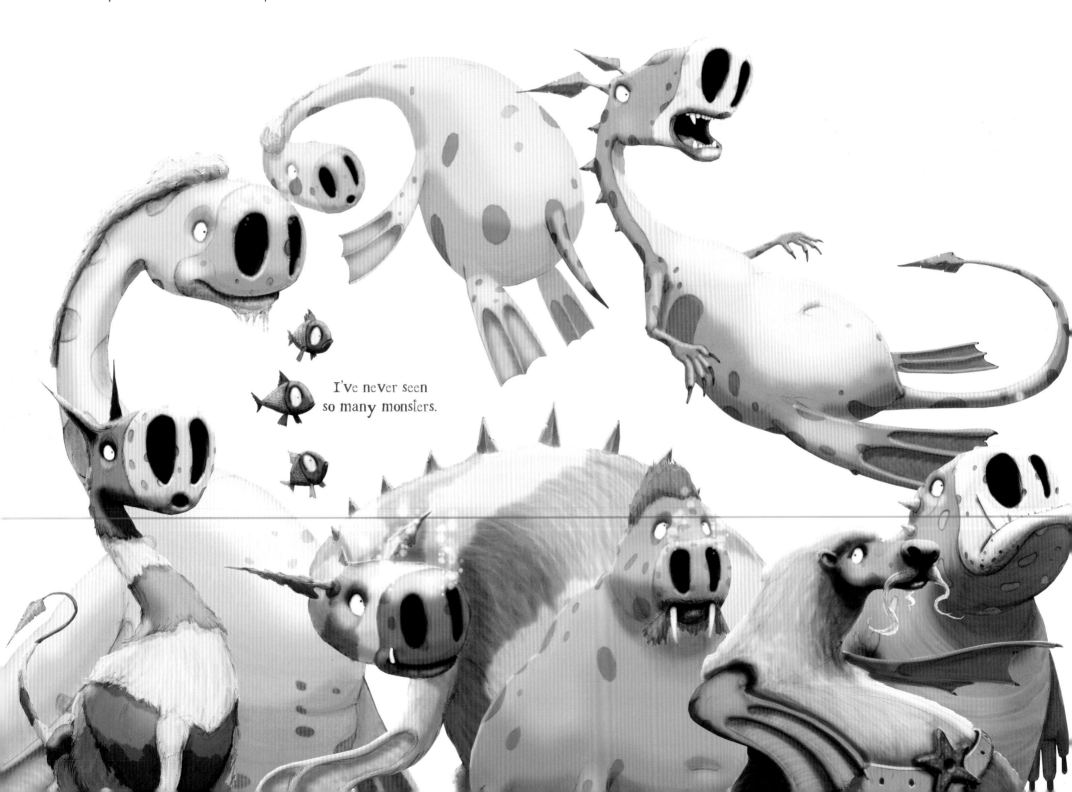

I've never seen so many monsters.

Don't be scared.

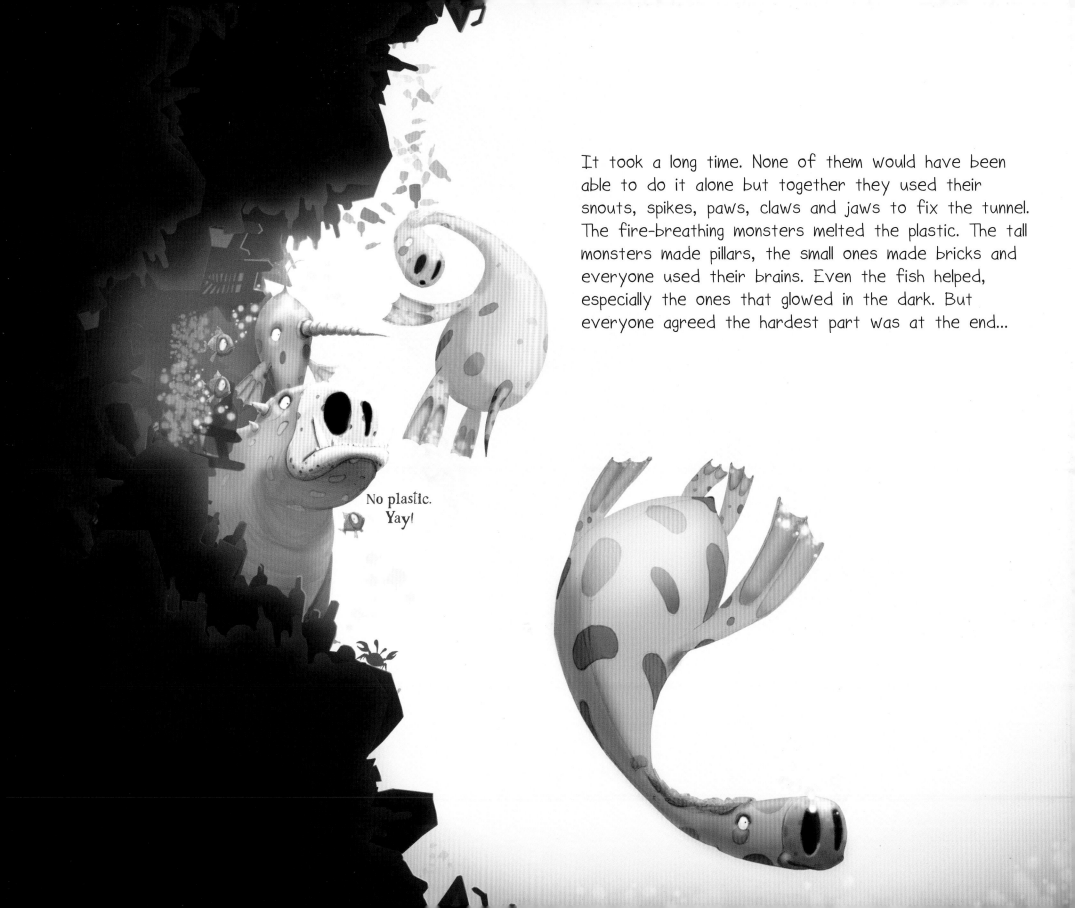

It took a long time. None of them would have been able to do it alone but together they used their snouts, spikes, paws, claws and jaws to fix the tunnel. The fire-breathing monsters melted the plastic. The tall monsters made pillars, the small ones made bricks and everyone used their brains. Even the fish helped, especially the ones that glowed in the dark. But everyone agreed the hardest part was at the end...

No plastic.
Yay!

...having to say goodbye.

Back home, Nessie was delighted to see her fishy friends. Above the water people were still out on their boats, but underneath something WAS different. "All the attention doesn't bother me now," Nessie thought. "I have holidays to plan and friends to visit. I wonder who I'm going to meet next?"

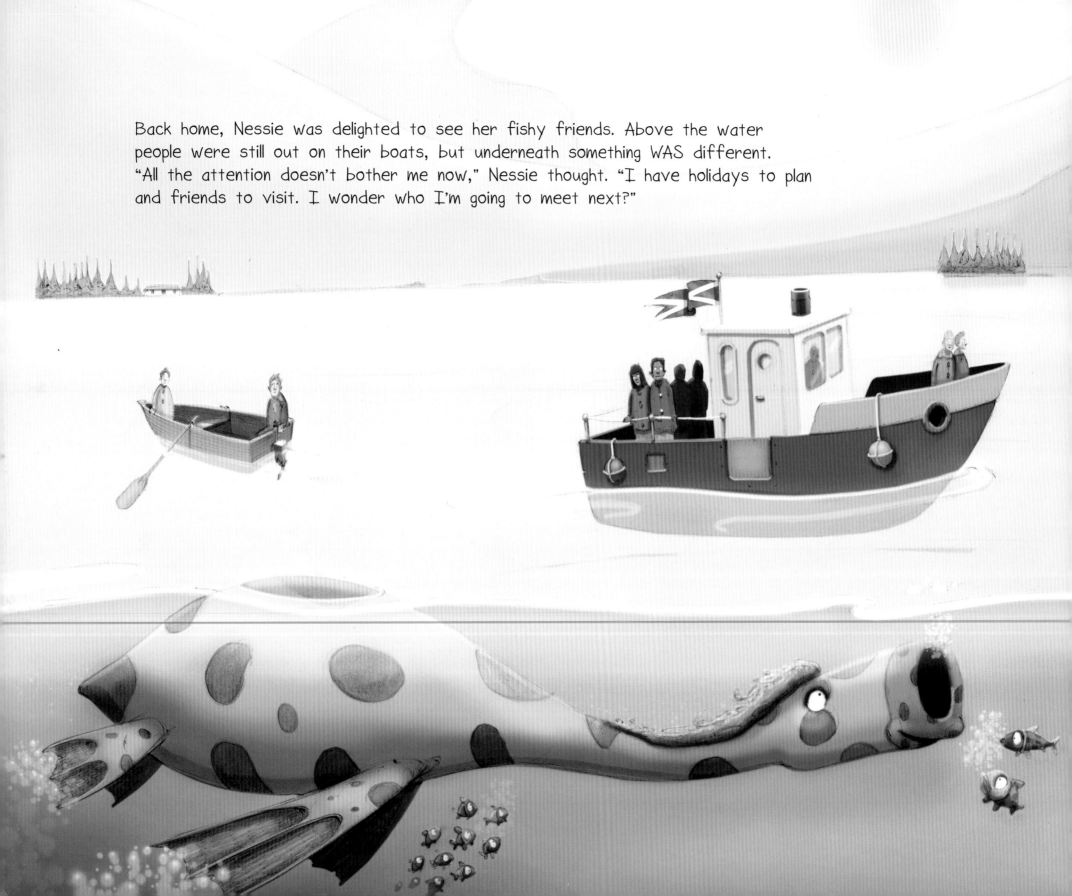

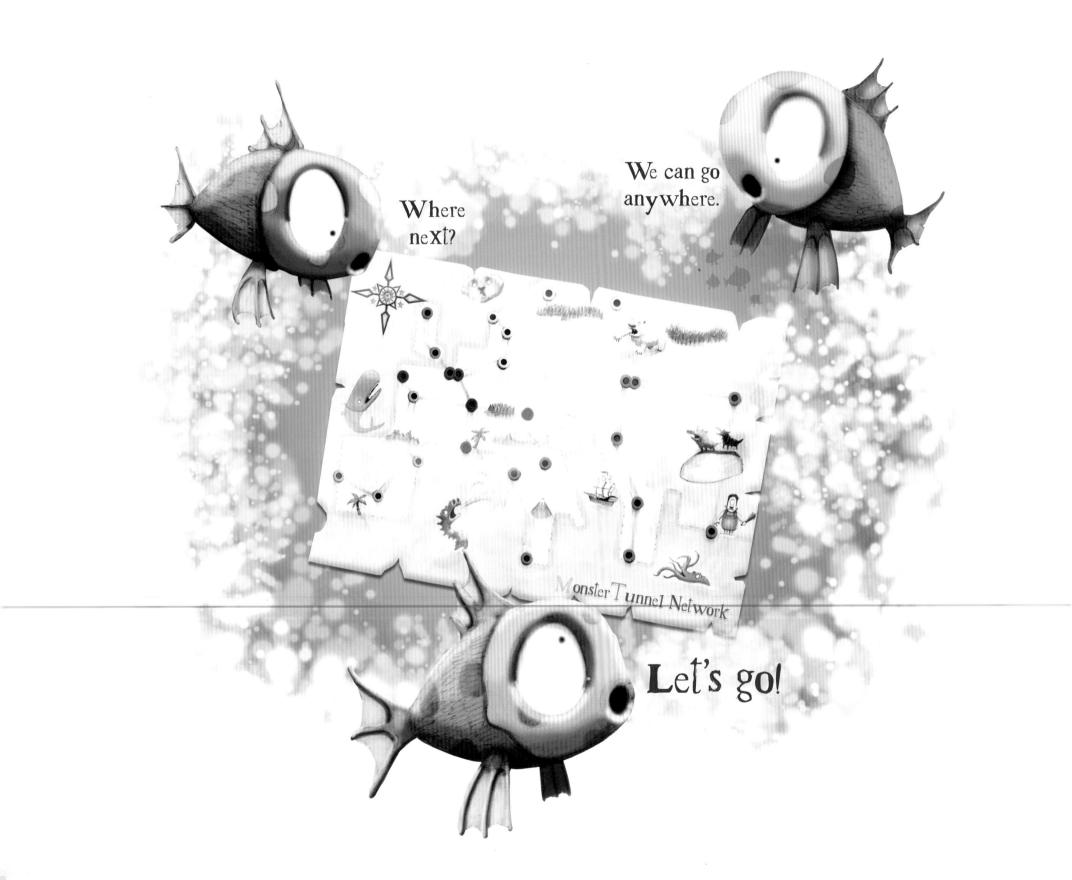